New YORK
USA

CHINA

MAY -- 04

This one's dedicated to all my cousins of the following families, with whom I shared the common ground
of growing up Italian in the Bronx: Nobisso, Zamboli, Siviglia, Tenore, Santoro, and De Falco,
and to the families who were our closest friends: Golfo, Mastropaolo, Reda, Freda, and Procaccino. –JN

To Michael and Philippe –DZ

Gingerbread House

602 Montauk Highway
Westhampton Beach, New York 11978 USA

S.A.N: 217-0760

Text copyright © 2002 by Josephine Nobisso
Illustrations copyright © 2002 by Dasha Ziborova

Art Direction by Maria Nicotra and Josephine Nobisso

Custom title font, Jennifer Dickert
Text fonts Eva Antiqua ensemble from DsgnHaus
Digitals by Dasha Ziborova
Manufactured by Regent Publishing Services Ltd.
The illustrations are rendered in cut paper collage and mixed media.
Printed in China

FIRST EDITION
10 9 8 7 6 5 4 3 2 1

Library of Congress Cataloging-in-Publication Data

Nobisso, Josephine.
In English, of course / written by Josephine Nobisso ; illustrated by Dasha Ziborova.-- 1st ed.
p. cm
Summary: Josephine tries to tell her new American class about her life in
Naples, Italy, but her teacher misunderstands what she is saying and thinks she grew up on a farm.

ISBN 0-940112-07-8 (Hard Cover) -- ISBN 0-940112-08-6 (Softcover)
[1. Schools--Fiction. 2. Immigrants--Fiction. 3. Domestic
animals--Fiction. 4. Italy--Fiction. 5. Humorous stories.] I. Ziborova, Dasha, ill. II. Title
PZ7.N6645 In 2002
[E]--dc21
2001002559

In English, of Course

Josephine Nobisso

Illustrated by Dasha Ziborova

Gingerbread House

Westhampton Beach, New York

"Welcome, boys and girls!" the teacher said, taking his globe from Josephine's desk, and giving it a smart spin. "Now that we've seen where we all come from, let's get to know one another. We'll try it in English, of course."

Josephine knew she was in trouble. Even though she *understood* most of the English she heard in the Bronx, she could not *speak* it well enough yet!

The teacher began, "Ling-Li, please tell us about China."
A tiny girl with an enchanting face made
the sweetest, quickest noises,

but Josephine wondered if she had
said anything in English at all.

"Juan," the teacher said to a boy, "talk to us about Puerto Rico."
Josephine decided that this boy was trying to speak Italian,

but that he needed more practice.

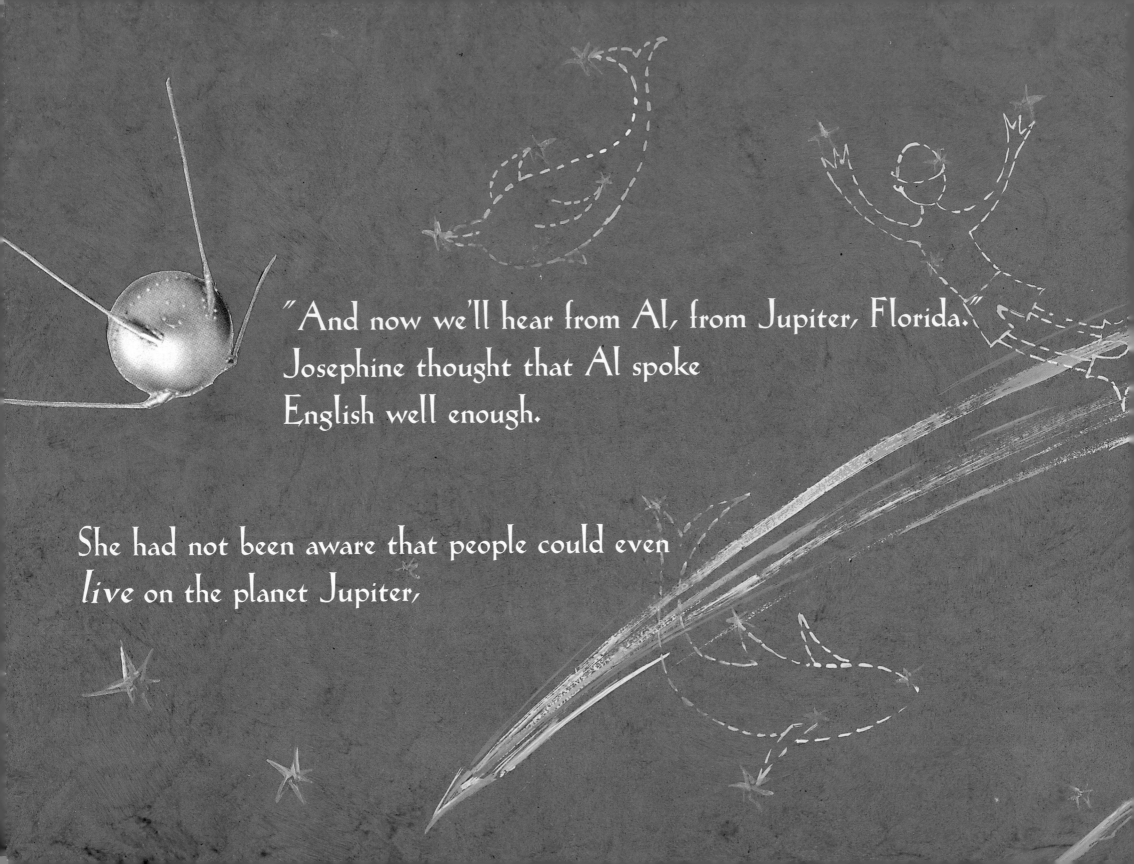

"And now we'll hear from Al, from Jupiter, Florida."
Josephine thought that Al spoke
English well enough.

She had not been aware that people could even
live on the planet Jupiter,

but Josephine had heard
enough English spoken
in the Bronx

to detect Al's
alien accent.

"Josephine," the teacher said, "it's your turn. Tell us about Italy."

"I come from *Napoli, Italia*," Josephine began.

So far so good. But Josephine had used up one of her best English sentences, and she had forgotten to make *"Napoli"* Naples and *"Italia"* Italy.

Well, maybe *not* so good!

"Did you live on a farm?" the teacher asked.
Didn't everyone know that *Napoli* was a magnificent city?
Josephine did not know the English words for "castles" or
"Roman ruins," or even "architectural engineers," which was
what both her parents were,

so she answered,

"I go to farm one time."

"Tell us about the farm, Josephine," the teacher said.

R i v e r

"Is many animals," Josephine answered, hoping she could recall enough English words from her little brother's new books to tell about her stay at the farm.

Pig

Cow

"Is cow...is *porco*—I mean pig...and is river."

"Was the cow your friend?"
the teacher wanted to know.

Josephine clearly saw the memory,
but unless the teacher helped her to
find the right English words, she would
not be able to tell it.

"Grass make cow green here." Josephine pointed.

"That's called the 'mouth,'" the teacher said.

Josephine nodded, grateful. "Mouth" was one of the words from her little brother's books!

"I holding neck of cow,
and when she walking, that cow, she do this to me."

Josephine grabbed a stuffed animal to show what she meant.

"We call that 'dragging,'" the teacher told her.

Josephine smiled. That was just the word she was looking for!

"I looking in mouth of cow, at grass,"
Josephine recalled, "and that cow, she give me this."

The teacher said,
"That's called 'a kick.'"

a pig

dRagging

kick

PORCO

mouth

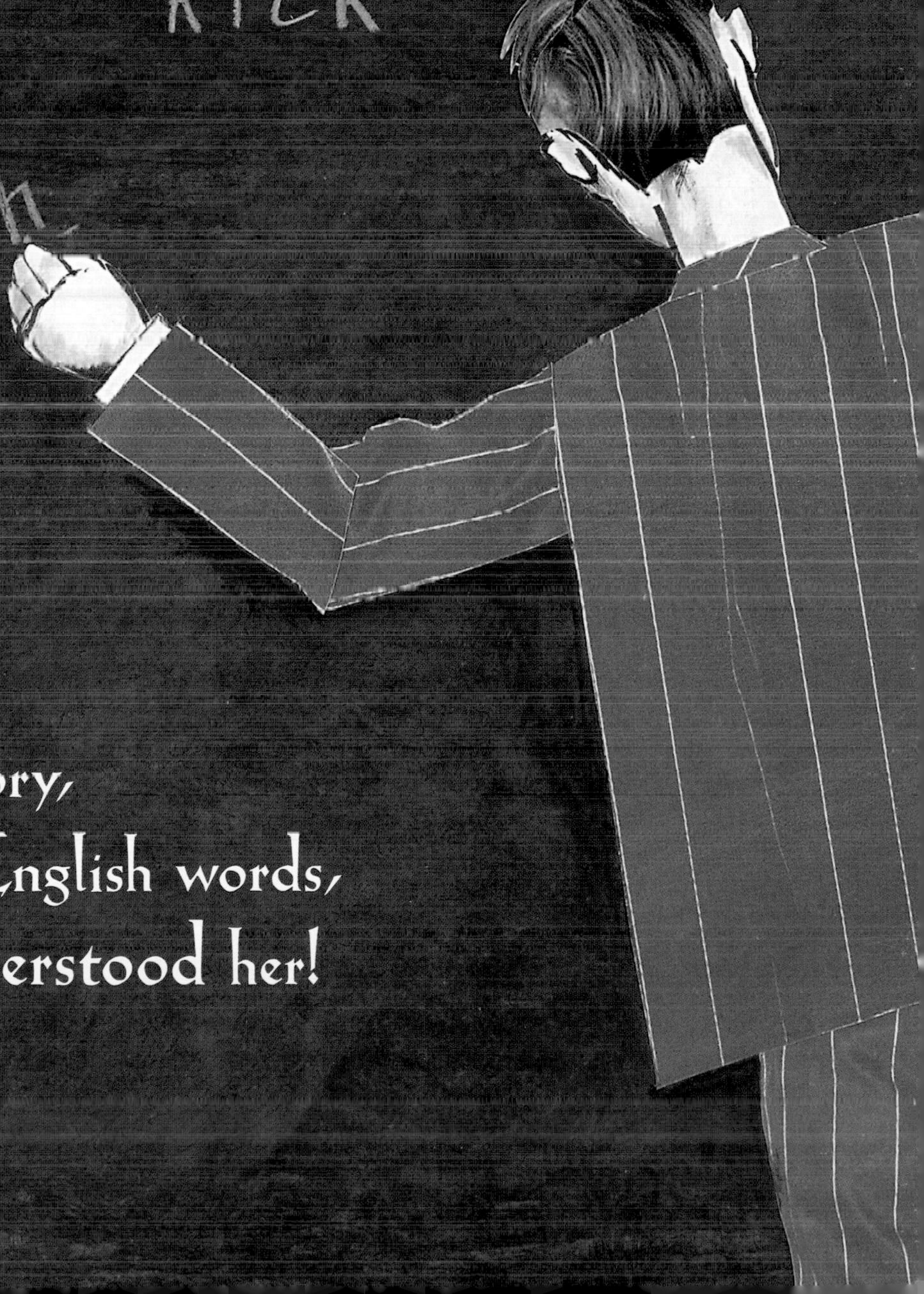

Josephine beamed.
She was telling a story,
learning some new English words,
and the teacher understood her!

"How about the pig, Josephine? Was he a little pig?"
Josephine shook her head. "No! Is big. Pig, he is big like car.

When pig coming, I do this."

"That's called 'hiding,'"
the teacher said.

"Yes! I hiding! So that pig, he no see me!

"If he see me, he give me this."

"That's called a 'push.'"

"Yes. And I do this."

"We call that 'falling down.'"

"Yes!" Josephine answered.

"So you never became friends with that pig?"

"Why I should be friends with that *porco*?"

The teacher smiled. "I see what you mean.
Do you want to tell us about the river?"

Ah! The teacher had now taught Josephine enough English words
to put the whole story together!

"When that cow she kick me,

I falling down in river.

That cow, she hiding,

but that pig, he push cow in river.

That river, it dragging us.

Much river in mouth.

I push me from river.

I dragging cow from river.

On grass, I looking in eyes of cow,
and cow, she looking in my eyes,
and that cow, she make
my hair all green.

"That cow, she no kick me no more."

"Oh!" the teacher said. "You had quite an interesting life

on the farm, Josephine!"

"I have no life on farm!" Josephine insisted.

"I go to farm *one* time!"

"Ah!" the teacher exclaimed. "I didn't understand everything at first!"

Josephine assured him, "Neither me!"

"We've learned a lot about you today!" he remarked,

giving his globe another spin.

"Tomorrow," Josephine promised, "I teach you about Naples, Italy."

"We look forward to that,"

the teacher said.

Josephine sat down, and copied from the chalkboard
all the new words her teacher had taught her.
Already, she was preparing tomorrow's story.
Tonight she would ask her parents how to say "castles"
and "Roman ruins" and "architectural engineers..."

in English, of course.

Author's Postscript

In English, of Course is based on experiences I had as a child. I was born in 1953, in the Bronx, a borough of New York City, to parents who had been raised in Italy. The Arthur Avenue section where we lived was dubbed "Little Italy," and it seemed that everyone there—the butcher, the baker, the ravioli-maker—spoke Italian. Our parents christened my sister and me with "Americanized" names, and insisted we speak English, the result being that (even when we became adults) they often spoke to us in Italian and we answered in English. When we were little, this English was quite "broken." If we wanted to express an emotion or event for which we did not know the words, my parents would urge us to make up an approximation. This contributed to my seeing words as being compliant to ideas, to my eventually "thinking" in smatterings of several languages, and to my having become a writer.

With no "English as a Second Language" programs in place, the crowded classrooms of that era often contained post-World War II immigrant children. My kind and hard-working teachers (at St. Martin of Tours, and later, at St. John the Evangelist, in Riverhead) managed to make me fall in love not only with the logic of grammar and with the phenomenon of verbal communication, but also with my family's adopted language itself.

Since 1990, I have been conducting about 100 presentations and workshops each year. During writing clinics in the method I have developed, I urge students to pursue a word when they think they've heard one that stands for a meaning they wish to express. A child asks a teacher, "What's that word for a round thing, like 'circle', but not 'circle', but a round thing that's full?" Her response, "Do you mean a 'sphere'?" helps the child to enter that word into his lifelong lexicon, just as, in our story, the teacher's "vocabulary prompts" help to introduce new words—or to reinforce familiar ones—for Josephine.

Even though neither of my parents was an "architectural engineer," as are Josephine's in our story, I used this narrative device to illustrate that native-speaking people sometimes underestimate the talents, dignity (and wit!) of newcomers to a country. When my father, the son of café-keepers near Naples, immigrated to the United States at the age of 28, he stood on the sidewalks with other men, his manicured hands held out, so that employers could choose day laborers. Having broad, strong hands, he was chosen to lay bricks. After some exciting years of working on the skyscrapers of Manhattan, my father moved us to eastern Long Island, where he became a successful building contractor. When he died in 1993, I wrote In English, of Course, a quiet homage that I share with you. Even now, when I pass a cottage onto which my father built a chimney, or glimpse the estates of celebrities like Steven Spielberg and Alan Alda, where his fancy stonemasonry remain, I smile, recalling that even though people who first heard his heavily-accented English sometimes assumed less of my father's abilities, his work stands as a testament to them—etched in stone, as it were.

Grazie! Ciao!